THIS BOOK BELONGS TO

You can write your name here.

Lohita 12-12-18

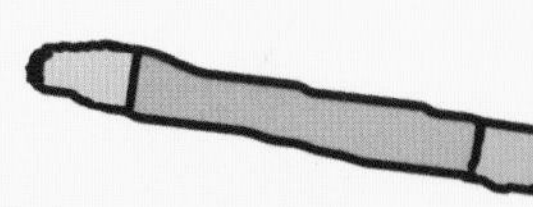

To SCHOOL CHILDREN EVERYWHERE . . .
just like ME!

Junie B.'s ~~Esenshut~~ Essential Survival Guide to School

(with some help from Grampa Frank Miller.)

RANDOM HOUSE NEW YORK

Hello, school children!

Hello! Hello!

It's me . . .

JUNIE B., FIRST GRADER!

And guess what?

You and I have a LOT in common!

'Cause wait till you hear this . . .

I am a real actual school child~~ren~~ myself!!!

REALLY!

I am NOT kidding!

I have been going to school for over one and a half entire years! And that is a long time to be in the system, I tell you!

I have learned a LOT OF STUFF from my teachers since I started school.

Here is **SOME OF THE STUFF** I have learned . . .

FIRST, I learned how to PRINT MY LETTERS AND NUMBERS. (I do a wonderful job in this area.)

NEXT, I learned how to read **WITHOUT MOVING MY LIPS**. (That is called lip reading, I believe.)

+ − SPELLING

AFTER THAT, I learned to do MATH and ~~SPELING,~~ and ART and MUSIC . . . plus also other subjects.

But that is not ALL!

THIS YEAR, I am learning how to get along with every single person in my whole entire classroom! (Except not the ones I don't actually care for, of course. 'Cause that would be ridiculous.)

WAIT A MINUTE!

Here is the BESTEST PART OF ALL!

And it is called . . .
I have ALSO learned OTHER information about school that no one even MEANT to teach me!

I AM NOT MAKING THAT UP, PEOPLE!

I have learned a jillion helpful hints that will help you SURVIVE at school. (SURVIVE is the grownup word for make it out alive.)

AND SO NOW . . .

I AM GOING TO PASS THIS INFORMATION ON TO

(Right in this EXACT BOOK, I mean!)

But you do not even have to thank me.

'Cause you are a school child~~ren~~ just like me.

And us school children have to stick together.

(Please turn the next page to begin.)

CONTENTS

CONTENTS

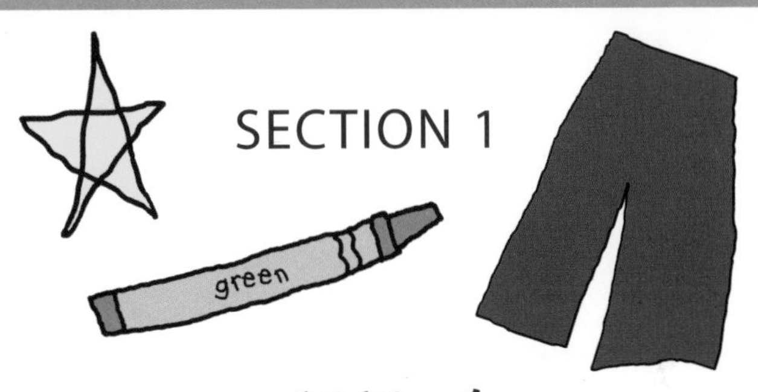

SECTION 1

GETTING STARTED

(Stuff you need to know and buy for school.)

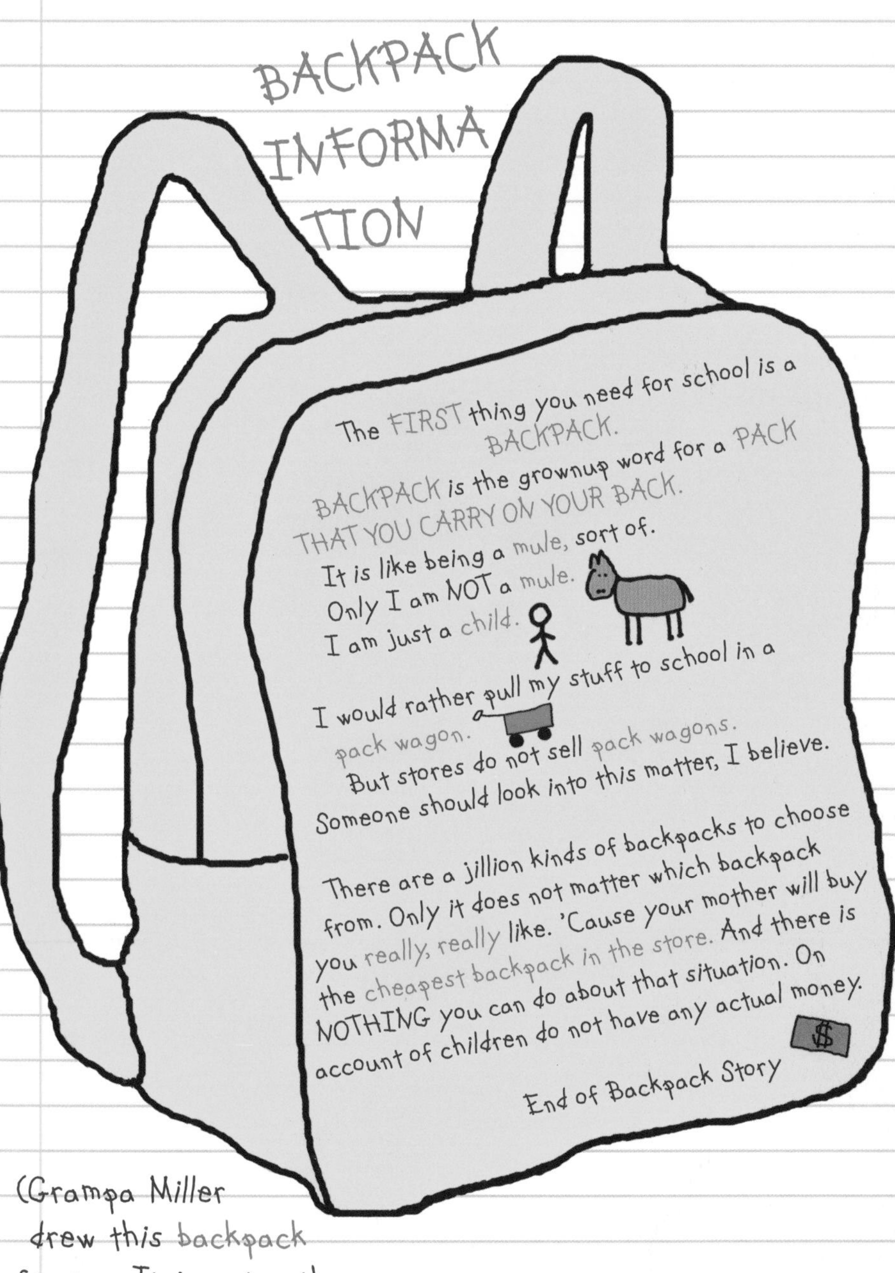

BACKPACK INFORMATION
The FIRST thing you need for school is a BACKPACK.
BACKPACK is the grownup word for a PACK THAT YOU CARRY ON YOUR BACK.
It is like being a mule, sort of.
Only I am NOT a mule.
I am just a child.
I would rather pull my stuff to school in a pack wagon.
But stores do not sell pack wagons.
Someone should look into this matter, I believe.
There are a jillion kinds of backpacks to choose from. Only it does not matter which backpack you really, really like. 'Cause your mother will buy the cheapest backpack in the store. And there is NOTHING you can do about that situation. On account of children do not have any actual money.
$
End of Backpack Story

(Grampa Miller drew this backpack for me. It is cuter than my backpack in real life.)

BACKPACK STUFF AND HOW MUCH IT WEIGHS

Some of the stuff that you carry in your backpack feels very light.

But OTHER stuff feels **so heavy** that you can't even pick it up, hardly.

Like one time I got a VERY BAD NOTE from my teacher. And that note felt **so heavy** that I couldn't even carry it home, almost.

Plus it was NOT EVEN MY FAULT!
On account of I was just playing at recess.
And I was **pretending to be a bull** with horns.
And so naturally I butted a girl (named May) with my head.
'Cause that is just what bulls DO, for heavens sake.

BULLS BUTT PEOPLE.

I did NOT make up that rule.

Only too bad for me. Because May is a tattletale girl.
And she ran and told my teacher.
And then he wrote this EXACT NOTE to my mother.
And I had to carry it home in my backpack.

Dear Mr. and Mrs. Jones,

Please speak to Junie B. about her "bullish" behavior today on the playground.

Thank you,
Mr. Scary

This note felt like it weighed a MILLION JILLION pounds, I tell you.

I am NOT KIDDING.

A BAD NOTE can BREAK YOUR BACK.

But HURRAY!

There is some HAPPY news about notes, too!

'Cause sometimes if you are PERFECT for a WHOLE ENTIRE DAY . . . your teacher gives you a note with a HAPPY FACE ON IT! And that is just a JOY I tell you!

A happy note feels as light as a feather in your backpack!

Dear Mr. and Mrs. Jones,

Please talk with Junie B. about her wonderful day in school today!

She was a model student!

You should be VERY proud of her!

Happy day!
Mr. Scary

Ha! Yay me!

THE HEAVIEST STUFF IN YOUR BACKPACK

A **BAD NOTE** from your teacher feels like you are carrying a hugie big HIPPO-POT-OF-SOMETHING. And a hugie big HIPPO-POT-OF-SOMETHING is a heavy load, I tell you!

HARD HOMEWORK in your backpack feels like you are carrying a big giant HOG on your back. And a big giant HOG is as heavy as a HIPPO-POT-OF-SOMETHING!

BUT . . .

A BAD REPORT CARD is the **HEAVIEST LOAD OF ALL!** Because A BAD REPORT CARD feels like you are carrying a whole entire ELEPHANT in your backpack!

(And THAT cannot be good for your spine.)

THE LIGHTEST STUFF IN YOUR BACKPACK

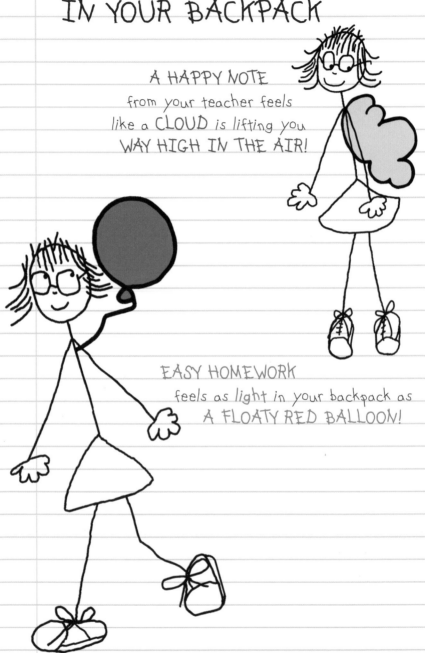

A HAPPY NOTE
from your teacher feels
like a CLOUD is lifting you
WAY HIGH IN THE AIR!

EASY HOMEWORK
feels as light in your backpack as
A FLOATY RED BALLOON!

But A GOOD REPORT CARD
is the lightest thing of all!

Because A GOOD REPORT CARD feels
like you're carrying a backpack full of
FLUTTERFLIES!

I LOVE THIS
HAPPY FEELING!

SOME STUFF ABOUT CLOTHES

Clothes ~~is~~ are something else that you need for school.

I would like to wear **pajamas** to school. But Mother says it is against the law.

One time—just to fool her—I wore my **pajamas** under my clothes.

That is called **PULLING A FAST ONE.**

It was not actually fun.

I sweated like a pig hog.

I will not be doing that again, probably.

IMPORTANT INFORMATION I HAVE LEARNED ABOUT SCHOOL CLOTHES

1. The bestest kind of clothes have **GIANT POCKETS** in them.

GIANT POCKETS are like having grocery bags sewed right on your clothes.

One time I was walking home from school and I found a little potato on the sidewalk.

I do not know how it got there.

But it fit into my pocket beautifully.

I took it home for dinner.

Mother would not cook it.

That was wasteful of her, I believe.

2. It is **ALWAYS** good to match the clothes you are wearing with **what you are having for lunch.**

That way—when you spill stuff—it doesn't even show that much.

The bestest color for clothes is DARKISH REDDISH. Darkish reddish is the color of chili and meatballs and ketchup.

DEMONSTRATION
HERE IS A CLOTHES ~~DEMONSTRASHUN~~
OF SPILLING STUFF.

This is a GIANT SLOP OF CHILI that I spilled on my white pants. You can see the slop very clear.

This is a MEATBALL that rolled off my plate and onto my yellow pants. I could not help that problem. Meatballs roll. That is just a fact of round meat.

But **HA!** Here is a whole entire PACK OF KETCHUP that I accidentally squirted on my lap. Only what do you know? My pants were **darkish reddish!** And so you can't even SEE it, hardly! I would like to shake the hand of the person who invented DARKISH REDDISH.

BORING DUMB SCHOOL SUPPLIES

Here is a list of school supplies that the school sent to Mother.

This stuff is **BORING**, I tell you!

I would rather buy **fun stuff** for school.

But Mother bought every **DUMB** thing on this list.

And so **THAT** is where **ALL THE MONEY WENT.**

SCHOOL SUPPLY CHECKLIST

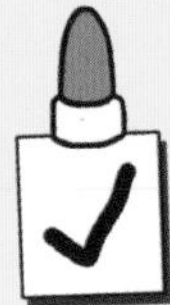

BORING DUMB WASHABLE GLUE

BORING DUMB RULER

BORING DUMB TISSUES

BORING DUMB ERASER

BORING DUMB #2 PENCILS

BORING DUMB SAFETY SCISSORS

BORING DUMB LINED PAPER

BORING DUMB PAINT SET

MY OWN FUN CHECKLIST

Here is a list of **FUN SCHOOL SUPPLIES** that me and Grampa Frank Miller drew.

Buying **STUFF LIKE THIS** would make school shopping a pleasure.

TEENSY LITTLE FLYSWATTER

What child couldn't use a teensy little flyswatter for heavens sake?

A teensy little flyswatter would come in very handy at school. On account of there is always someone who needs a teensy swat.

And that is just a fact.

SOFTIE FAKE BULL HORNS

Okay. This one doesn't even NEED explaining.

Pretending to be a bull is half the fun of recess.

BIG GIANT FISHING BOOTS

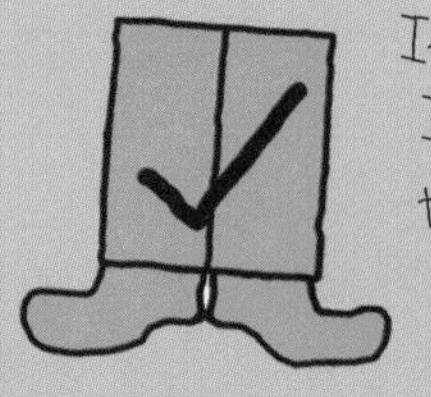

If I had BIG GIANT FISHING BOOTS, I could splash and jump in puddles on the playground, and I wouldn't even get my feet wet.

Also I could splash water on May. THAT would be just plain fun!

TWO IMPORTANT THINGS YOU SHOULD ~~MEZMORIZE~~ memorize

Here are TWO IMPORTANT THINGS you should always ~~mezmorize~~ memorize before you go to school . . .

1.) FIRST . . . ALWAYS KNOW YOUR NAME.

Knowing your name is VERY IMPORTANT. On account of teachers ALMOST ALWAYS make you print a NAME TAG. (I do not know why this is.)

BUT . . .

if (for some reason) someone has **not** told you your name by the time you go to school, here is A SIMPLE SOLUTION!

Just make up your favorite name that you would **like** to be called and put THAT on your NAME TAG!

HA!

My favorite NAME TAG would look like this.

If I was a boy, I would like this name tag, I think.

Okay . . .

2.) Now here is THE SECOND thing you need to know.

ALWAYS KNOW YOUR AGE.

YOUR AGE is how the office knows WHAT GRADE to put you in. And so—if you do not know your age—this could be a problem.

Like if you are 6 . . . but you think you are 12 . . . they will put you in middle school. And that would NOT be good. On account of middle school children are biggish and tallish.

Plus also they have a bad attitude.

And so here is ANOTHER SOLUTION I thought of!

If you do NOT know how old you are, just say,

I'm 6!

You really cannot go wrong with that age.

'MERGENCY STUFF FOR YOUR BACKPACK

Here is an important **HEALTH TIP** for you.

It is called **DO NOT LEAVE HOME WITHOUT**

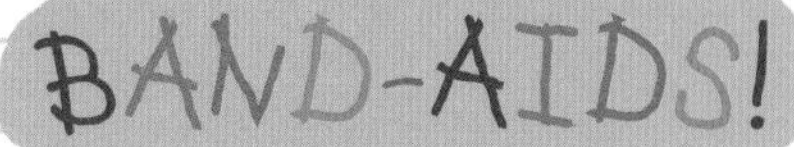

'Cause here are the facts.

Children fall down on the playground a very, **VERY** lot.

That is because there are DANGEROUS GRASS CLUMPS out there!

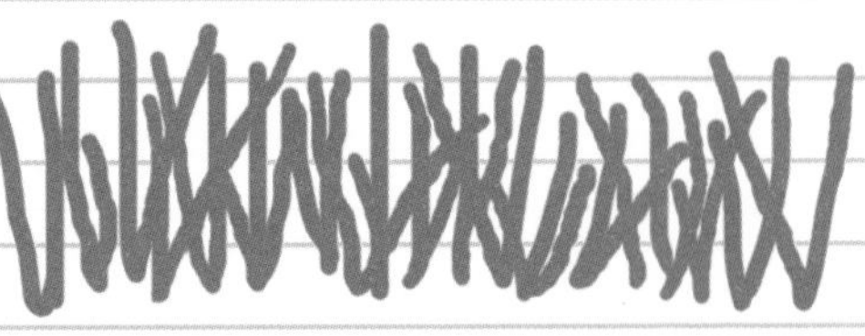

Sometimes when I trip over a DANGEROUS GRASS CLUMP, I scrape my knee.

That is no big whoop, usually.

But one time . . .

KERTHUNK!

I hit my head on some **hard dirt**!

It did not actually hurt that much.

Also, it did not bleed.

But still . . . I quick reached into my backpack.
And I pulled out a Band-Aid.
And I slapped it right up there.

Then I shouted . . .

STAND BACK, PEOPLE!
I JUST CRACKED MY WHOLE ENTIRE HEAD OPEN!
IF ANYONE TOUCHES THIS BAND-AID . . .
MY BRAIN WILL COME EXPLODING OUT!

Everyone backed away.
Little children are very nervous about exploding brains.
That was an enjoyable moment.

(Here is a nice assortment of Band-Aids that you can put on an exploding brain.)

Blue Circle

Red Triangle

Green Square

Yellow Rectangle

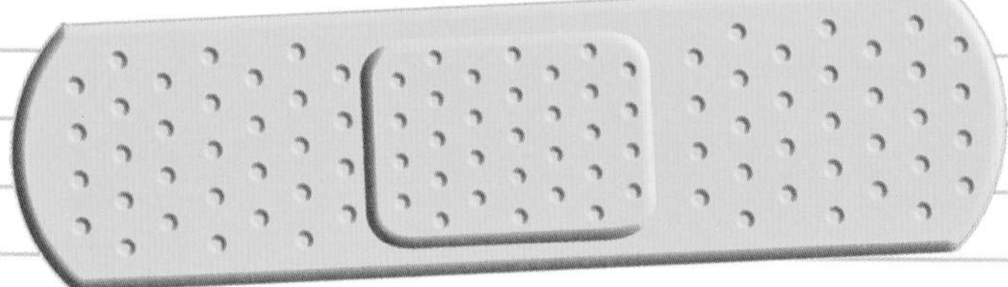

Plain Old Normal Kind

Extra Stuff That Maybe I Forgot

Okay, so here is what I'm thinking . . .

I'm thinking that maybe there is stuff about GETTING STARTED at school that you would like to ADD TO MY BOOK!

Like maybe you would like to draw a picture of YOUR OWN BACKPACK, possibly.

YES! That is a GREAT IDEA!

Here is a space for you to draw that exact item!

Plus here is room for you to draw YOUR VERY OWN FAVORITE CLOTHES!

But WAIT!
Here's an even FUNNER idea!

You can write some silly school supplies that YOU would love to buy!

SECTION 2

GETTING THERE

(All of the ways I can think of to get to that place.)

THE **WORST WAY** I CAN THINK OF TO GET TO SCHOOL IS CALLED

WALKING!

WALKING means **exactly** what it sounds like.

FIRST you go out your front door.

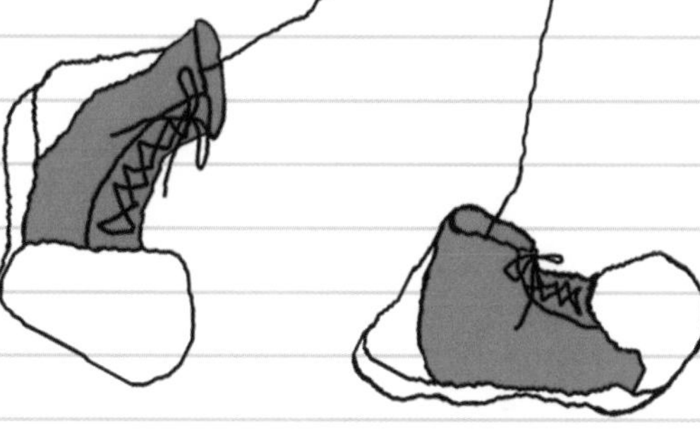

THEN

you just

keep

putting

one foot

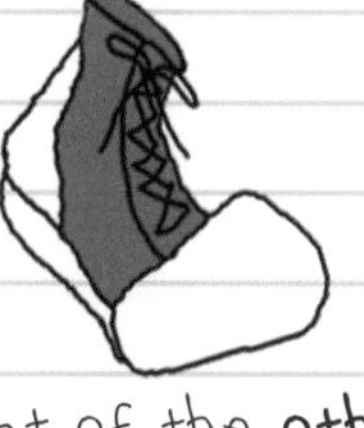

in front of the **other** one

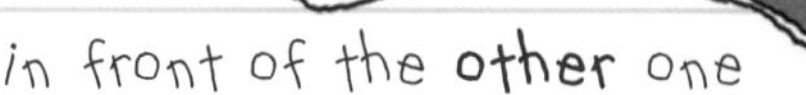

AND the **other** one

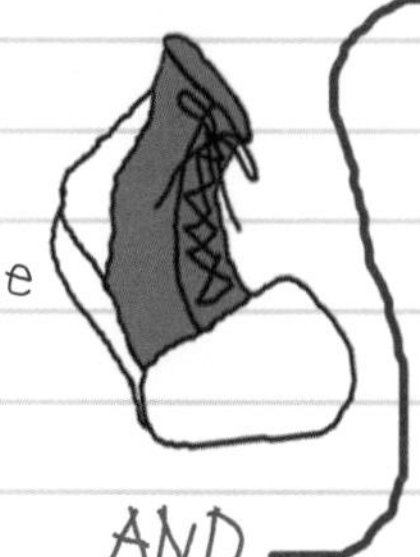

AND

AND the other one

AND the other one

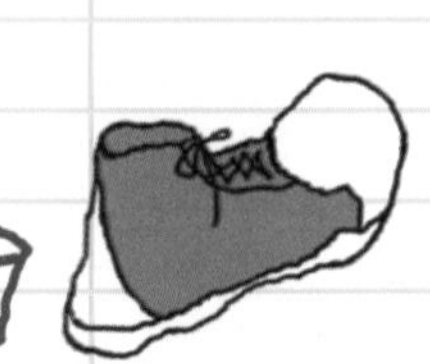

the other one

→ UNTIL YOU FINALLY GET TO SCHOOL!!!

I am NOT kidding!

Children are STILL doing this **ridiculous activity**!

Walking is how CAVEMAN CHILDREN got to school for heavens sakes.

BUT WAIT! HOLD IT!

WALKING is not the ONLY WORST WAY to get to school.

There is ALSO . . .

RIDING YOUR BIKE!

RIDING YOUR BIKE means exactly what it sounds like, too.

FIRST you go out of your house.

THEN you get on your bike.

And you just keep pedaling and pedaling and pedaling until you FINALLY GET TO SCHOOL!

Here is a picture of pooped legs after they pedal to school.

(Frank Miller drew the bike and all the shoes.)

(I drew the pooped legs.)

THE WAY I PERSONALLY GET TO SCHOOL IS CALLED **RIDING THE BUS.**

Here is how you do it.

1. Go out your door.

2. Walk to wherever your bus stops.

3. Then wait and wait and wait and wait for the bus to get there. Plus also wait for the door to open.

4. Get on the bus.

5. Then sit and sit and sit and sit while your bus driver takes you to school.

It is a **LOT** of sitting, I will tell you that.
But at least it's better than WALKING or RIDING YOUR BIKE.

BUS RULES

There are **MANY** rules about riding the bus.
I am very familiar with them.

When I grow up, I might be a bus driver, possibly. When the children are being nice, I will smile and say Good morning, children.

BUT if the children are **NOT** being nice, I will do a frown. Then I will holler HEY! I HAVE HAD IT WITH YOU PEOPLE! IF YOU DON'T BE QUIET, I AM DRIVING THIS BUS STRAIGHT TO THE COUNTY JAIL!

This saying would work very well with children, I believe. On account of my friend Sheldon visited his Aunt Bunny at the County Jail. And he said everybody there has to wear an orange jumpsuit.

Sheldon says that most people do not look good in orange.

And so here is my suggestion . . .
If you don't look good in orange, you should follow the RULES OF THE BUS.

(I will make a list of them for you.)

RULES OF THE BUS

NUMBER 1.

When your bus driver is driving the bus, do not jump up and start yelling,

FASTER! FASTER! FASTER!

I have had an actual experience with this rule. On account of one time, I thought it would be amusing to yell FASTER. But my bus driver named Mr. Woo did not laugh.

Instead, he sent a bus note home to my parents. It was called BUS WARNING NUMBER ONE. They did not get a kick out of it.

Bus Warning Number One:

Today your child:

Junie B. Jones

misbehaved on the bus. After 3 warnings, she will no longer be able to ride with us.

Please talk to her about her behavior today.

Mr. Woo

NUMBER 2.

Do not press your nose and lips on the window and make faces at the people driving in cars.

Some of these people are **NOT** good sports.
One time a lady took a picture of me doing this activity.
She took it with her cell phone.
Then she emailed it to Principal.

I do **NOT** think people should be allowed to take pictures while they are driving.
That is just plain DANGEROUS.

I would like to have that lady hauled off to jail.

MORE RULES OF THE BUS

NUMBER 3.

Do NOT NOT NOT pour chocolate milk from your thermos on the head of the person in front of you!

On account of a boy named Clifton did this to a boy named Ronald. And Ronald had to wear chocolate milk on his head for the whole entire day.

PLUS . . .

Now Clifton is not allowed to bring chocolate milk in his thermos for the whole rest of the year.

AND . . .

Also he had to dry clean Ronald's shirt and buy him shampoo.

That was a good lesson for all of us on the bus.

We learned a lot about the price of dry cleaning.

NUMBER 4.

Do NOT play TICKLE on the bus.

Even though TICKLE is NOT the same as fighting . . . someone always ends up on the bus floor. (That cannot be helped.)

But then what do you know?

You get ANOTHER NOTE sent home by the bus driver.

Bus Warning Number Two:

Today your child:

Junie B. Jones

misbehaved on the bus.
This is her second warning.
After 3 warnings, she will
no longer be able to ride
with us.

Please talk to her about
her behavior today.

Mr. Woo

CONCLUSION
And so in ~~CONKLUSHUN~~ . . .
Here are ALL THE THINGS YOU SHOULD
DO WHEN YOU RIDE THE BUS.

SIT STILL!

BEHAVE YOURSELF!

AND BE GLAD YOU'RE NOT WALKING!

Period.

End of Bus Rules.

SOMETIMES parents DRIVE their children to school.

There are 2 reasons for this, usually.

REASON NUMBER 1.

The FIRST reason parents drive you is because your bus comes very too early and your mother and daddy are sleepyheads. Sleepyheads sleep WAAAAY too late. Then they quick spring up. And they rush you out the door. And they drive you to school in their pajamas.

REASON NUMBER 2.

The SECOND reason parents drive you is you were supposed to take the bus. But you accidentally spilled your cereal down the front of you at breakfast. And then you accidentally danced with Teddy instead of changing your clothes. And so you accidentally missed the bus.

And Mother had to drive you.

This situation has happened in my own actual life.

Mother was NOT pleasant in the car that day.

This was Grouchy Mother's ~~conservation~~ conversation.

HOUSE

Did you remember to bring your homework? Or were you too busy dancing with Teddy?

Stop poking your brother.

If you don't stop poking your brother, I am driving this car to the County Jail.

It looks like someone was so busy dancing that she forgot to comb her hair.

Have a nice day.

SCHOOL

(I never should have told her Sheldon's story about the County Jail.)

CARPOOLING

Some children get to school by CARPOOLING.
CARPOOLING is the grownup word for when different mothers and daddies take turns driving a bunch of children to school that they don't even KNOW, hardly.

CARPOOLING is one of the **biggest disappointments** of my whole entire school career.
On account of one time, Mother and Daddy said we were going to try CARPOOLING instead of taking the bus.
And so the next morning the CARPOOL was going to pick me up.
That is how come I put on my bathing suit.
Plus also I got a towel.

Only WAIT till you hear this!

THERE WAS NO ACTUAL POOL IN THE CAR!
And so what kind of mean joke was THAT, I ask you?

HERE is what I THOUGHT my CARPOOL would look like.

HAPPY HAPPY CHILDREN!

HAPPY HAPPY MOTHER!

HAPPY HAPPY DAY!

BUT . . .
HERE is what my CARPOOL actually looked like.

And so here are TWO QUESTIONS I keep wondering:

1. Why do they call it a CARPOOL if there IS NO POOL?
2. And WHY can't grownups just call stuff what it really is?

CARPOOL should be the grownup word for SOMEBODY GOT STUCK DRIVING A BUNCH OF KIDS TO SCHOOL . . . AND THEY ARE NOT HAPPY ABOUT IT.

I would ALMOST rather walk a million kajillion miles to school than **CARPOOL** with some **BIG GROUCH.**

One million kajillion miles to school
Only one million miles to go

(Well . . . ALMOST . . . but NOT quite.)

RIDING PIGGYBACK

Okay . . . here is the honest truth.
RIDING PIGGYBACK to school is just a little joke that me and Grampa Frank Miller thought of.

Here is what that would look like, probably.

That is a hoot!

OTHER SILLY WAYS

I can think of a jillion OTHER SILLY WAYS that I could get to school, too.

Like maybe I could get FIRED OUT OF A CANNON!

Or else maybe I could ~~PARASHOOT~~ PARACHUTE OUT OF AN AIRPLANE!

(I asked Grampa Miller to draw me in a parachute. But he had to go fix the upstairs toilet. And so I am going to give this space to you again!)

Draw ANY SILLY WAY YOU WANT to get to school!

SILLY WAY NUMBER ONE!

SILLY WAY NUMBER TWO!

SECTION 3

GETTING BOSSED AROUND

(Some of the bossy bosses who will boss you.)

PRINCIPAL

There are **many** BIG PEOPLE who will BOSS YOU AROUND at school.

This is just a fact of BIG PEOPLE.

BIG PEOPLE are BOSSY.

The BIGGEST BOSS is named PRINCIPAL.

PRINCIPAL is the KING OF THE SCHOOL.

(Except he does not actually wear a ~~crayon~~ crown.)

PRINCIPAL lives in a little room all by himself.

It is called

I do not think it is good to live in a little room all by yourself. That can make you crazy, I believe.

PRINCIPAL'S JOB

Okay. Here is the thing.

No one actually **knows** what PRINCIPAL does.

All that children know for a **positive fact** is that . . .

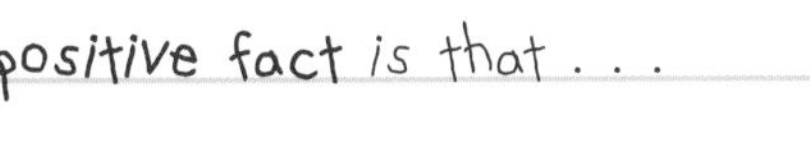

1. PRINCIPAL can be a **man** or a **woman**, and
2. PRINCIPAL **wanders** and **lurks**.

My PRINCIPAL is a man.
He does not have hair on the top of his head.

This condition is called BALDIE MAN. Only do NOT call him BALDIE MAN to his face. On account of PRINCIPAL does not have a good sense of humor about this situation. (I learned this information the hard way.)

Here is a picture that me and Grampa drew of PRINCIPAL.

Here is some hair he would look more attractive in, I think.

OKAY . . .
NOW we need to talk about the WANDERING and LURKING problem.

PRINCIPALS WANDER and LURK all over the school.
LURK is the grownup word for hanging around without a purpose.
Sometimes PRINCIPAL lurks in the hall.

BUT wait till you hear THIS!
Sometimes PRINCIPAL wanders right into your EXACT CLASSROOM!
Then EVERYONE sits up STRAIGHT AND TALL!
Even your TEACHER, I mean!
On account of—if PRINCIPAL does not like how people act—he can FIRE them from school!
I am NOT kidding!
He can FIRE CHILDREN!
AND ALSO he can FIRE TEACHERS!

That is why we MUST ALWAYS BE ON THE LOOKOUT FOR PRINCIPAL!

OH! WAIT!
And here is the OTHER THING I need to tell you!
If you do NOT behave yourself in class, your teacher will send you to THE OFFICE to TALK TO HIM!
But BIG SURPRISE!
PRINCIPAL NEVER wants to talk about the weather or birds or your dog.
Oh nooooo . . .
PRINCIPAL ONLY wants to talk about WHY ARE YOU BAD.
Only you are NOT BAD!
You just made a MISTAKE!
(And so here is an idea of how to cover your face so no one can see you while you're waiting to talk to PRINCIPAL.)

(It is called the old Sweaterhead Trick.)

Another **BIG BOSS** at the school is **JANITOR.**

JANITOR is the name for the guy who **HAS THE KEY TO EVERY SINGLE ROOM IN THE WHOLE ENTIRE BUILDING!**

I am **serious!**

Being **THE BOSS OF KEYS** is even more important than being **PRINCIPAL.** On account of if **JANITOR** doesn't unlock the school every morning, then **PRINCIPAL** will not even have a **JOB!**

When I grow up, I would like to be the janitor at my school.

I will call myself **JANITOR GIRL.**

(Here is a picture of that event.)

The **JANITOR** at my school is named **GUS VALLONY.**

GUS VALLONY fixes stuff and **cleans** stuff and **paints** stuff and **builds** stuff and **patches** stuff and **shines** stuff. He has a million tools in his closet. He can open stuff that no one else can open.

ALSO he has **sponges.**

I enjoy sponges a very **very** lot.

I drew this picture of **GUS VALLONY'S CLOSET.**
I put some extra stuff in there for him.
He would like these extra items, probably.

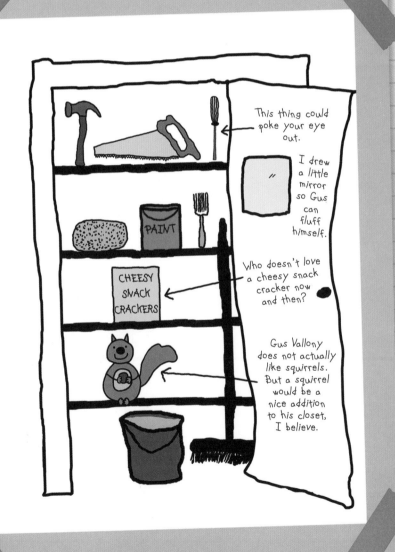

This thing could poke your eye out.

I drew a little mirror so Gus can fluff himself.

PAINT

CHEESY SNACK CRACKERS

Who doesn't love a cheesy snack cracker now and then?

Gus Vallony does not actually like squirrels. But a squirrel would be a nice addition to his closet, I believe.

TWO OTHER BOSSES

Okay. Here are 2 other important BOSSES that you'll need to know.
First, there is my FAVORITE!

1. THE BOSS OF COOKIES

At my school, the BOSS OF COOKIES is
MRS. GLADYS GUTZMAN.
GLADYS is the BOSS of THE WHOLE ENTIRE COOKIE OPERATION.

She MAKES them . . .
She BAKES them . . .
And then she BRINGS them to the little children.

GLADYS GUTZMAN is the
BESTEST BOSS
in the whole school!

Here is a picture I drew of her. I made her out of sugar cookie shapes.

(I am not actually allowed to call her Gladys, by the way.)

The OTHER important BOSS you need to know is

2. THE BOSS OF SICK KIDS

THE BOSS OF SICK KIDS is called THE NURSE.
THE NURSE is also THE BOSS OF HURT PEOPLE.

I am going to be honest with you.
This is **NOT** as good a job as THE BOSS OF COOKIES.
Children like THE NURSE a lot.
But we like THE BOSS OF COOKIES **way better.**

My SCHOOL NURSE is named
MRS. WELLER.
I made a picture of her out of
Band-Aid shapes.
That is because she patches you up
if you hurt yourself.
Also—if you have a headache—she lets you
lie down on her couch. Then . . . after you
feel better . . . she makes you go back to
your room.
(I don't care for that part of the treatment.)

Mrs. Weller knows if you are **really sick**
or if you are just **faking it.**
I do not know HOW she knows.
But she ALWAYS, ALWAYS KNOWS.

So be careful of SCHOOL NURSES, people.
SCHOOL NURSES are sharp as a tack.

TEACHERS—BOSSES OF Y-O-U!

TEACHERS are THE BOSSES of Y-O-U and Y-O-ME.

TEACHERS are the people that actually teach you. That is how they came up with the name TEACHERS probably.

TEACHERS boss you around **every single minute** of the day.

They tell you **where to sit** and **when to stand** and **where to play** and **when to talk** and **when to be quiet**.

Here is how my teacher sounds when he BOSSES ME around.

JUNIE B. NICE!
JUNIE B. QUIET!
JUNIE BEHAVE!
JUNIE B. POLITE!
JUNIE B. SEATED!

B. is an easy initial to boss around.

On account of B. makes a sentence out of every bossy thing I can think of.

I would like to have the initial W.

'Cause JUNIE W. NICE doesn't sound like bossing.

JUNIE W. NICE doesn't even make sense, in fact.

Here are some **HELPFUL HINTS** to follow if you don't want to get BOSSED so much.

You should

BE NICE!
BE QUIET!
BEHAVE!
BE POLITE!
BE SEATED!

If you can do ALL of those things
EVERY SINGLE DAY,
you are waaaaay better than me.

TEACHER THE FIRST

So far I've had two different teachers.
My TEACHER THE FIRST was my kindergarten teacher.
Her name was MRS.
She had another name, too.
But I just like MRS. and that's all.

MRS. had longish hair.
She was very nice.
Here are some of the things I remember about her.

1. Sometimes she stared at me a real long time.
2. Sometimes she sat me at a table all by myself.
3. Sometimes she marched me to THE OFFICE.
4. Sometimes she looked at me and took aspirin.

Now that I think about it, maybe Mrs. wasn't that nice.

Here is a picture of Mrs. taking aspirin.

I am giving her water.

That is very thoughtful of me.

TEACHER THE SECOND

This year I have my TEACHER THE SECOND.

His name is MR. SCARY.

Only he is not even **scary**.

He is NICE, NICE, NICE!

MR. SCARY enjoys me.

I can just tell.

Sometimes he takes aspirin, too. But I am not to blame for that . . . probably.

I still get hollered at. But that is just natural.

Also, MR. SCARY does not always holler with his voice.

Sometimes he hollers with **his eyebrows**.

It is very interesting to watch that.

On account of even though his voice is silent . . .

I can hear him hollering **loud and clear**.

Here is what EYEBROW LANGUAGE looks like.

JUNIE B. QUIET!

What? That wasn't you?

It was that mean girl May?

Sorry, Junie B. I should have known that it wasn't you.

STUFF ABOUT YOUR BOSSES

That is ALL THE STUFF I can think of about my SCHOOL BOSSES.

But guess what?

I bet that you probably have DIFFERENT TEACHERS and BOSSES than me.

And so . . .

HERE is space for YOU to draw or write about them!

Draw or write WHATEVER YOU WANT! 'Cause HA! I am NOT THE BOSS OF YOU!

SECTION 4

GETTING IN TROUBLE

(Plus how to stay out of it!)

NOTES

(AND SOME OF THE REASONS YOU GET THEM)

Okay, I am going to be HONEST again.
I get LOTS of notes sent home.
I am not talking about HAPPY NOTES either.
I am talking about NOT HAPPY NOTES.

Here are some of my NOT HAPPY NOTES.
NOT HAPPY NOTES are NOT fun.
But they can be VERY colorful.

Junie B. had a little tussle on the playground.

Please talk to Junie B. about her behavior in music.

I'm sorry to say that Junie B. did not have a good day.

I am sorry to tell you that Junie B. was shooting straws at the lunch table again.

NAMES YOU SHOULD NOT CALL PEOPLE . . . PROBABLY

LAST YEAR there was a boy in my class who was NOT NICE to me.

NOT NICE to me AT ALL I mean!

I called him MEANIE JIM.

Also I called him THAT JIM I HATE and YOU BIG FAT JIM and STUPID HEAD JIM.

These names were **not appropriate,** apparently.

I got a BACKPACK FULL of NOTES sent home.

Also—at the end of kindergarten—I found out that MEANIE JIM ACTUALLY LOVED ME!

And so THAT was a whole year WASTED!

I learned A LOT about name calling in kindergarten.

Kindergarten was a real EYEBALL OPENER.

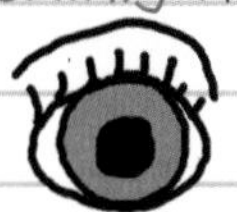

This year I do **not** like a girl named TATTLETALE MAY. Her other name is BLABBERMOUTH MAY.

It is NOT my fault that these are her names.

On account of—if May does not want to be a tattletale—all she has to do is keep her BIG YAP SHUT.

WHOOPS . . . HOLD IT.

Grampa Frank Miller said I am not allowed to say YAP.

He said I have to think of NICER NAMES.

I told him I would give it a try.

NICER NAMES

I have been thinking about **NICER NAMES** for a very long time.

Here is what I came up with . . .

NAMES That I Should NEVER EVER Call People.

1. YOU ICKY BIG POOHEAD BOY
2. YOU GIANT BLABBERMOUTH GIRL
3. YOU STINKY STINKBOMB
4. YOU DIRTY ROTTEN RATTY PANTS

INSTEAD . . .

I Should Call Them These NICER NAMES.

1. YOU BOY WITH THE HEAD I DON'T ACTUALLY CARE FOR
2. YOU GIRL WHO I DON'T WANT TO HEAR ANOTHER PEEP OUT OF
3. YOU PERSON WHO I DON'T WANT TO SMELL AT THIS PARTICULAR TIME
4. YOU TEENSY LITTLE HAMSTER PANTS

I am going to work REALLY hard on saying NICER NAMES.

I do not want to disappoint Grampa Frank Miller.

Also I like the name HAMSTER PANTS.

MORE STUFF ABOUT NOTES

TEACHERS are TATTLETALES.

That is just a fact of teachers.

Every time you do something wrong, they write A NOTE to your mother and daddy.

If you don't give THE NOTE to Mother and Daddy, the teacher calls your house during dinner and stirs up more trouble.

Some notes are shortish.

Shortish notes are for when teachers can tattletale in one sentence.

Mr. and Mrs. Jones,
Junie B. enjoys butting people with her head a little more than we'd like.
Mr. Scary

Mr. and Mrs. Jones,
Junie B. would like
to tell you about
poking people with
her pencil eraser.
Mr. S.

Mr. and Mrs. Jones,
Please ask Junie B.
about the lunch tray
incident.
Mr. S.

Longish notes are for BIGGER STUFF.

Like one time I accidentally clunked May on the head with my lunch box.

Only it wasn't even a BIG CLUNK (like **KERTHROPP**).

It was just a little clunk (like kerplinkie).

But still she tattletaled to Mr. Scary.

And so **THAT** is how come at recess I pretended to be a SUPERHERO while I was swinging.

And when May walked past . . . I SPRANG down on top of her.

And then both of us rolled and rolled in the softie grass.

Plus also we laughed and laughed.

Except not actually May.

INSTEAD . . .

That mean girl TATTLETALED on me again.

And whoopie do.

Big surprise . . .

I got a LOOOOONGISH NOTE sent home.

From the Desk of Mr. Scary

Dear Mr. and Mrs. Jones,

Junie B. has been working very hard on her self-control issues. In the past few weeks, she has shown a lot of progress. But today was not a good day.

At lunch, she hit May in the head with her lunch box. May was not harmed. As Junie B. explained it, "It was not a big clunk. It was a little clunk." But as I told her, regardless of the "clunk level," we do not like to see this behavior from her.

Later, at recess, Junie B. tackled May from the swing set. Again, May was not harmed. This time, Junie B. said she was pretending to be a superhero. When I told her that superheroes do not tackle small girls, she said that May was "not a little girl." May was "a giant lizard from another planet."

Junie B. has a wonderful imagination and spirit. But we need to keep reminding her that she needs to control them.

Please talk to her about today's behavior. When you have finished, please sign this note and have her return it to me tomorrow.

Thank you for your help.

Sincerely,
Mr. Scary

Susan Jones

(signed) Susan Jones/Robert Jones

(This note did NOT make my life easier.)

I wish I could write a note to my teacher's mother.

If I could write a note to Mr. Scary's mother, here is what I would say.

From the Desk of
Junie B., First Grader

Dear Mr. Scary's Mother,

I do not know why you named your baby Mr. Scary. That is an odd name for a baby, I think. But it is none of my business.

Here is why I am writing you a note.

Your son Mr. Scary writes too many notes.

I don't know where he learned this activity. But he does not know how to control himself.

If I accidentally forget to give the notes to Mother and Daddy, he calls my house and stirs up trouble.

Please tell him he is not allowed to write any more notes for the rest of the year. If he does not mind you, please take away his pen ~~privges.~~ privileges

Thank you.

Your friend,
Junie B., First Grader

P.S. Hello to your husband, whatever his name is.

DUMB SCHOOL RULES

SCHOOL RULES are the main reason children get in trouble.
If SCHOOLS didn't have RULES, then no one could break them. And everyone would have a nice day.

Here are 3 SCHOOL RULES I wish we didn't have.

1) NO BUTTING PEOPLE IN THE STOMACH WITH YOUR HEAD.

What kind of dumb rule is this, I ask you?
How are you supposed to pretend you're being a bull at recess if you can't butt children in the stomach with your head?
Being a bull is good for the 'magination.

That is all I have to say about bulls.

2) NO RUNNING IN THE HALLS.

This is a **dumber rule** than the NO BUTTING PEOPLE WITH YOUR HEAD rule.

'Cause RUNNING is the BESTEST exercise you can do.

Halls are MADE for running.

They are always the right temperature.

Plus they do not have DANGEROUS GRASS CLUMPS!

Teachers should NOT send you to THE OFFICE for **running in the hall**. Instead they should be happy you are getting exercise and get out of your way.

When children get their energy out, school is a calmer place.

That is just a fact of nature.

3) NO SWINGING ON THE SWINGS AND WAITING UNTIL TATTLETALE MAY WALKS BY . . . AND THEN JUMPING ON TOP OF HER ON ACCOUNT OF YOU ARE PRETENDING TO BE A SUPERHERO SAVING THE WORLD FROM GIANT LIZARDS.

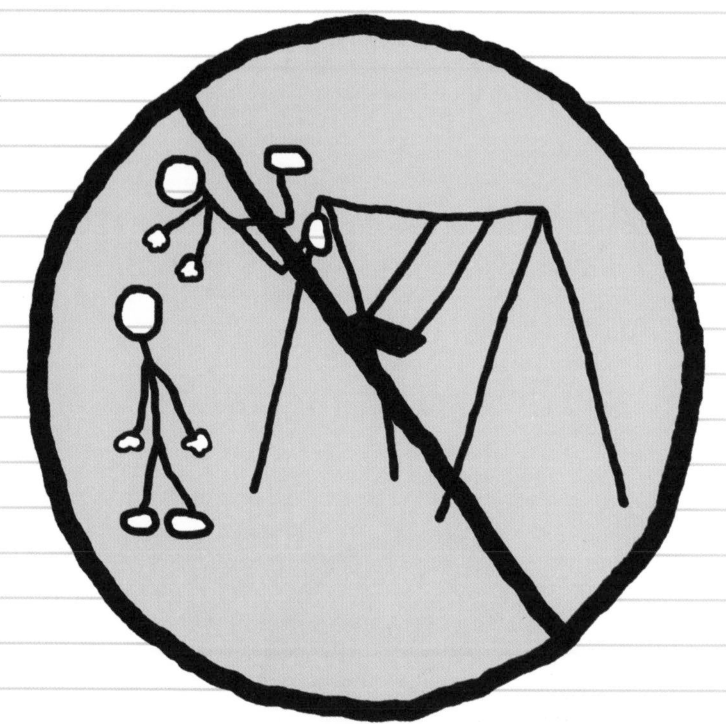

I should not actually have to discuss this one.
This is called a NO BRAINER.
If the world ends up with too many GIANT LIZARDS it is not my fault.
By the way . . . this was **NOT** in the school rules that got sent home to my parents by the PTA.
I had to find out about this rule ENTIRELY ON MY OWN.

RULES YOU HAVE TO FOLLOW AT THE LUNCH TABLE OR ELSE YOU GET IN TROUBLE

There are MORE RULES at the lunch table than you can ~~shape~~ shake a stick at.

Mr. Scary says that LUNCH RULES teach you how to be polite.

POLITE is the grownup word for do not blow milk out of your nose and other things of that nature.

Here are some LUNCH RULES that I try to remember.

1) DO NOT CHEW WITH YOUR MOUTH OPEN.

If you chew with your mouth open, people can see the chewed-up food in there.

This sign should be stuck on every lunch table at school.

Sometimes—when I see chewed-up food—I close my eyes and turn my head.

Other times, I holler . . . CLOSE YOUR MOUTH! YOU ARE MAKING ME SICK TO MY STOMACH!

(That is appropriate, I believe.)

2) NO SHOOTING STRAW PAPER AT PEOPLE.

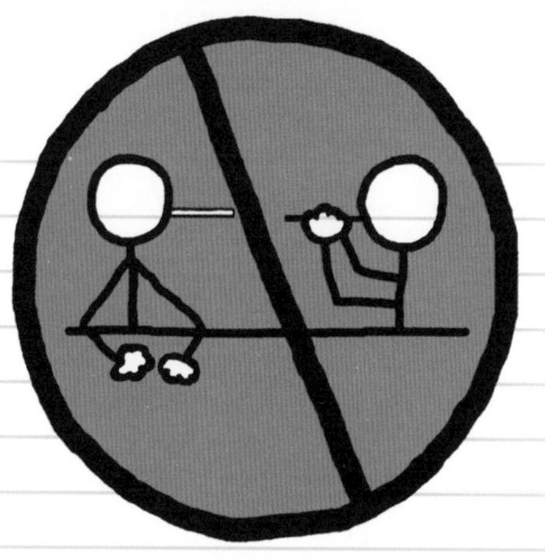

This is the ridiculousest rule I ever heard of.
Straw paper could not hurt a fly.
Not even if you hit him directly in the head.

3) NO HITTING PEOPLE IN THE HEAD WITH YOUR LUNCH TRAY.

Okay. Fine. This is probably a bad idea.
I only had to be yelled at once for this problem.
Plus it was not even my fault. On account of a GIANT LIZARD from another planet named May was walking by. And her LIZARD HEAD got in the way of my tray.
Mr. Scary did not actually believe that story.
I got another note sent home.

HOW TO STAY OUT OF TROUBLE

(Only I'm not actually an expert in this area.)

Here is an IMPORTANT SAYING from my Grandma Helen Miller:

THE EASIEST WAY TO GET OUT OF TROUBLE IS NOT TO GET INTO IT IN THE FIRST PLACE.

She says this same saying **every time** I bring a NOTE home.

I do not actually care for this saying. On account of HOW am I supposed to stay out of trouble when there are **a million rules** that I never even HEARD of?

Here is a sample of this problem . . .

Last week I was singing BINGO WAS HIS NAME-O during silent reading.

May tattletaled on me.

I stopped singing and I did loud humming instead.

Mr. Scary said for me to please stop humming.

I stopped.

Then I tapped out the tune on my desk with my pencil.

Mr. Scary came to my chair.
He gave me a note to take home.
He did not care that I never heard of the BINGO RULE before.

That man is a note writing machine.

Dear Mr. and Mrs. Jones,

Please speak to Junie B. about the importance of silent reading.

Silent reading does not include singing
BINGO WAS
HIS NAME-O.

Mr. S.

MORE RULES I DIDN'T KNOW ABOUT UNTIL I ACTUALLY GOT NOTES SENT HOME

The PTA should include these in their RULE BOOK.

1. Always raise your hand when you want to talk. If you do not get called on, do NOT climb on your chair and shout HEY! IS SOMETHING WRONG WITH YOUR EYES?

(This joke is not that amusing, apparently.)

2. Do NOT grit your teeth and make a GRR sound at your neighbor.

GRRRRR

3. Do NOT play the drums on your lunch box when there is a guest speaker.

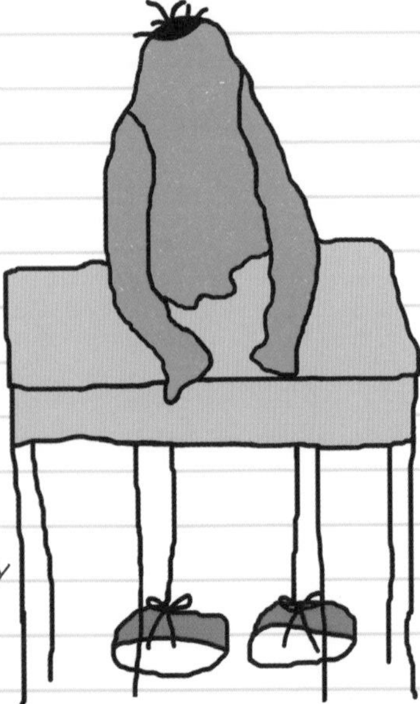

4. If your teacher says Get out your math book do NOT say Fat chance.

(Helpful hint: If you accidentally DO say Fat chance . . . quick hide your face.)

5. NEVER EVER copy your neighbor's homework.

(This is especially important if your neighbor did not do her homework, either.)

6. DO NOT NOT NOT NOT NOT peek at your neighbor's test paper. This mistake will get reported to PRINCIPAL and he will

PUT IT ON YOUR PERMANENT RECORD!

PERMANENT RECORD means that—when you grow up and you try to get a job—you will have to tell them that you **peeked at Herbert's spelling test.** If you don't tell them, you will get arrested.

(This is the way it was explained to me by May.)

7. Do NOT eat a ham sandwich during science.

(This one seems unreasonable to me.)

8. Do NOT tap dance on the way to the pencil sharpener.

9. If your teacher stops by your desk . . . do NOT say Please move along.

10. Do NOT take off your shoes and socks when you come in from the playground.

Not even if your feet are steamy hot and they really need fresh air.

11. Do NOT call your teacher the name of Buddy Boy.

12. Do NOT write MAY IS A STINKBOMB on the board.

(That is all the rules I feel like writing about now. But there are LOTS more, believe me.)

SOME CIRCLES FOR YOUR OWN STAY OUT OF TROUBLE RULES!

Here are some circles that me and Grampa Miller made for you!

Now you can draw your own **RULE PICTURES** just like I did!

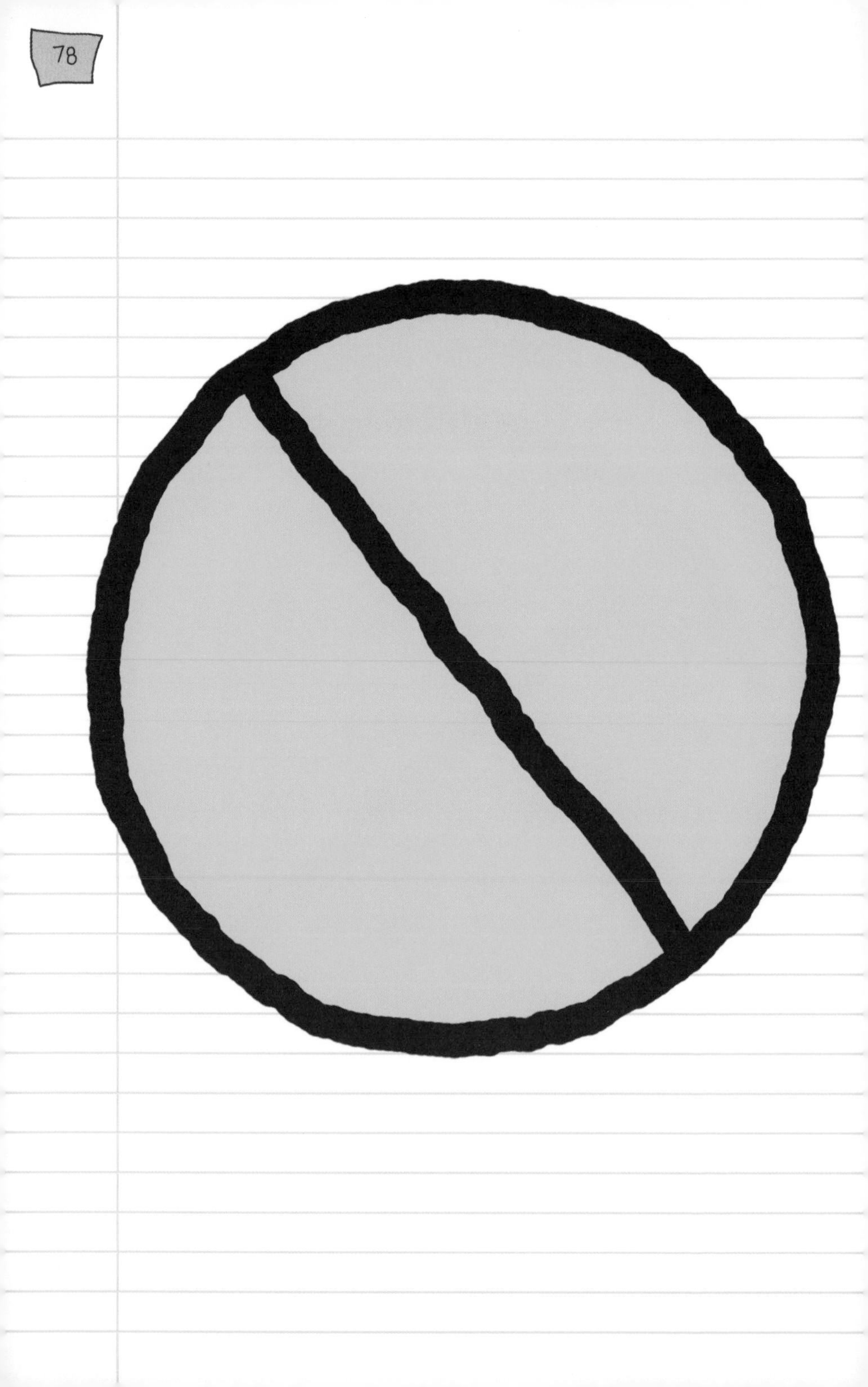

And here is some paper where you can

WRITE A NOTE TO YOUR OWN

TEACHER'S MOTHER!

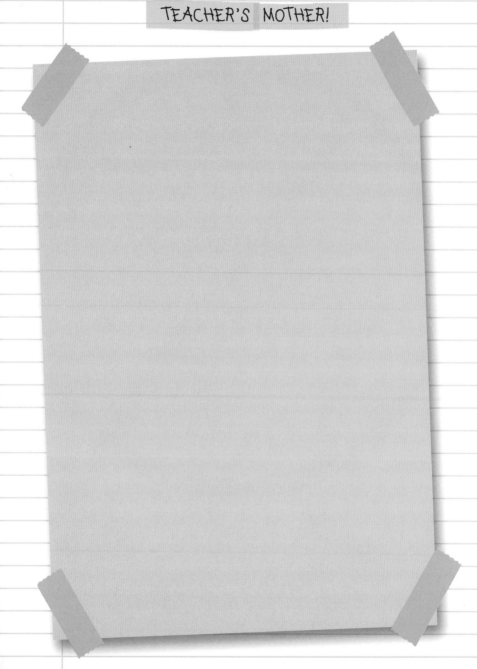

SECTION 5

A+ Satisfactory ✓+

GETTING GRADED

(Tests . . . plus homework . . . plus (GULP) report cards.)

B- F

Needs Improvement

D C

HOMEWORK IS ACTUALLY SCHOOLWORK

HOMEWORK is the name for

SCHOOL
WORK that
they make
you do at
HOME.

I do not actually **GET** this situation. On account of . . . if it is already named SCHOOLWORK then it should be done at school.

'Cause **HOME** is where you **DON'T** do WORK. Which is why it is called HOME and **not** SCHOOL! (That is just basic ~~vocavulary~~ vocabulary.)

But it doesn't even **matter** what children think about this situation. Because teachers give you SCHOOLWORK to do at HOME. And there is NOTHING we can do about it.

I am going to tape some of my real homework pages in this book.

I did **NOT** want to do **ANY of this work!**

I tried and tried to get out of it.
I grumped and grumped.
And I fussed and fussed.
And I grouched and grouched.

Then Mother said to **KNOCK IT OFF** or else I am

NOT getting LEMON PIE after dinner.

I knocked it off.
(Mother knows all my weak spots.)
Okay . . .
So here is a page of my MATH HOMEWORK.
I got a CHECK+ for it.

A CHECK+ means you **tried your best** to do **the whole entire page.**

A CHECK– means you did sloppy work and skipped a bunch of junk.
(This happens sometimes.)
Mother and Daddy only like it when I get a CHECK+.
They are difficult people to deal with.

Math Tables

Add the number at the top of the table to each of the numbers in the left column.

Add 5	
3	8
6	11
8	~~14~~ 13
5	10

I still think this might be right, possibly.

Add 7	
9	16
2	9
5	~~11~~ 12
8	~~14~~ 15

My brain got pooped when I got to these two.

Add 9	
10	19
7	~~17~~ 16
4	13
6	15

This one was a tuffy.

Here are 2 lemon pie plops that were on my fingers.

1 plop
+1 plop
2 plops

This is a page of SPELLING HOMEWORK that I (really) did not feel like doing. That is why I got the CHECK–.

Spelling Worksheet - #8

✓–
You can do better than this, Junie B.!

get	pet	men	met	ten
test	bed	best	say	today

Write each word three times.

1.	get	get	get
2.	pet	pet	pet
3.	men	men	
4.	met	met	
5.	ten		ten
6.	test	test	
7.		bed	bed
8.	best		best
9.	say	say	
10.	today		today

Put each of these words in a sentence.

say Say say.

rest Say rest.

stop Say stop.

met Say met.

today Say today.

HOMEWORK THAT I MIGHT LOVE, LOVE, LOVE . . . possibly

May says that she LOVES, LOVES, LOVES
to do homework.
I do not understand that opinion.
'Cause there is NO HOMEWORK that I would **ever**
LOVE, LOVE, LOVE to do.

Not unless it was FUN, FUN, FUNWORK . . . of course.

WHOA!
WAIT A MINUTE!
THAT was just a **BRILLIANT IDEA** of me, I think!

TEACHERS SHOULD GIVE CHILDREN
FUNWORK TO DO AT HOME!

YES! YES!
FUNWORK WOULD BE LIKE JUMPING ON
YOUR BED!

Or else maybe it could be EATING LEMON PIE!

HA!
If HOMEWORK WAS FUNWORK I WOULD
LOVE, LOVE, LOVE TO DO IT!

THIS would be my first FUNWORK assignment!

JUMPING ON THE BED

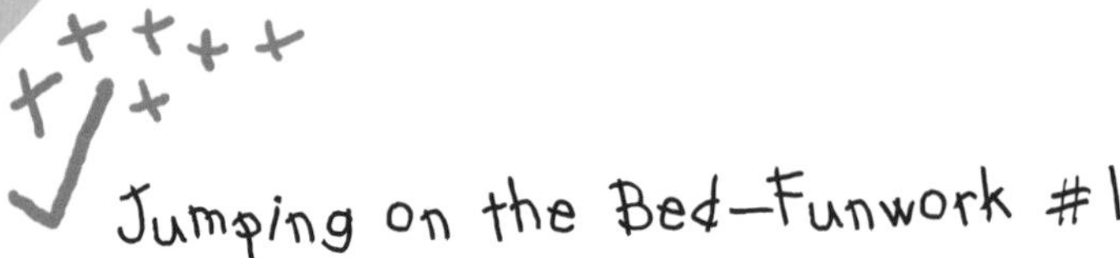

1. Please go home and jump on your bed.
2. Jump as high as you can!
3. Jump and jump and jump and jump and jump!

Put a check every time your head bumps the ceiling.

YUM! This would be my second FUNWORK assignment.

EATING LEMON PIE!

Eating Lemon Pie—Funwork #2

Eat pie.
Here is how.

1. Step one.

2. Step two.

3. Step three.

Check here if you fit it all into your mouth in one bite.

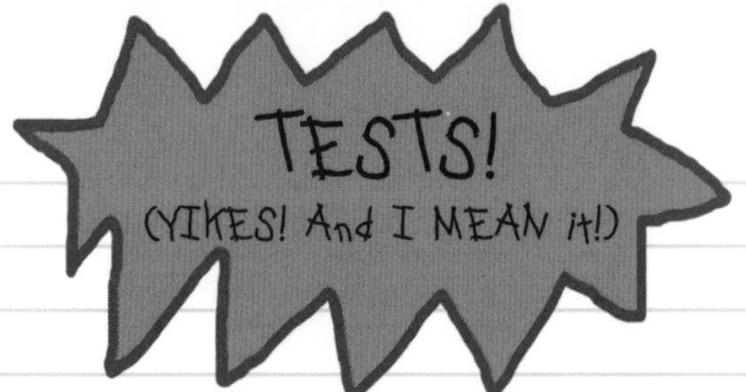
TESTS!
(YIKES! And I MEAN it!)

TESTS is the school word for when teachers teach you stuff. Only **they don't believe** that you actually learned anything. So they **pass out questions for you to answer** so you can **prove** you remembered something.

TESTS ARE NOT FUN.

When a test is getting passed out, children feel PRESSURE in their heads.

Also their hands get wettish.
And their throats can't swallow that good.

That is how you feel for the whole entire time the test is on your desk, by the way.
Then finally you finish.
And you hand it in.
And your teacher takes it home and puts a grade on it.

GRADE is the school word for TEST LETTER.
I do **not** know why they don't just call it TEST LETTER. But that is not the way their minds work.

HERE ARE ALL THE GRADES YOU CAN GET ON A TEST.

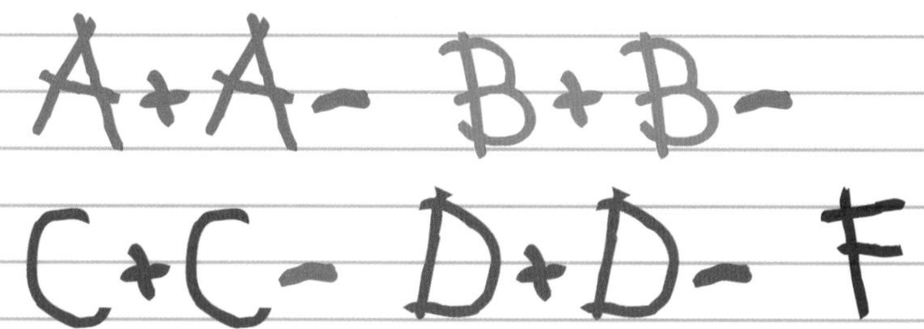

F does not come with a + or a -.
I do not know why.

A+ is the bestest grade that you can get.
That kind of grade makes parents smile
as big as they can.

B+ makes them smile, too.

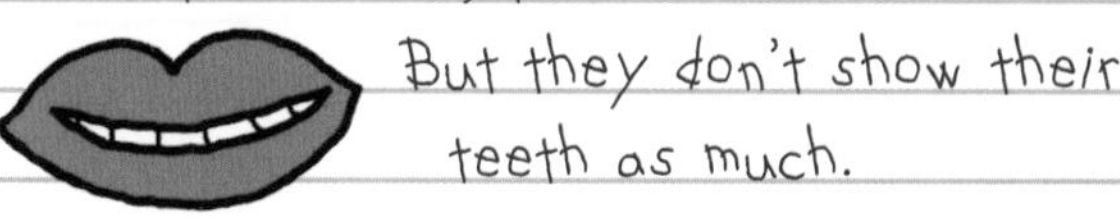

But they don't show their
teeth as much.

If you get a C they just look at you.

With a D or F they suck their cheeks way
into their heads.
You do not even want to **see** what **this** face looks like.

Last week I had a science quiz.

Quiz is the school word for it's ~~eggzactly~~ exactly like a test only shorter.

I only got ONE wrong.

But ONE wrong was a B-.

I don't know how that is possible.

B–

Junie B. Jones

"Our Solar System" Quiz

Please circle the correct answer.

1. There are ____ planets in our solar system.
   (a) 6 (b) 5 (c) 8 (d) 12

2. The Earth completes one orbit around the ________ in 365 days.
   (a) moon (b) stars (c) planets (d) sun

3. The planet closest to the sun is:
   (a) Earth (b) Mars (c) Mercury (d) Venus

(I do not actually know how I fell for this one.)

4. The moon has many deep holes called:
   (a) moon pies (b) craters (c) sinkholes (d) gulches

5. The sun is really a:
   (a) planet (b) moon (c) star (d) comet

If I was a teacher, THIS is the kind of quiz I would give on the solar system.

If teachers gave this kind of quiz, children would **never** feel **sick** or **sweaty**. I am positive of that.

A+ "Our Solar System" Quiz

Please circle the correct answer.

1. Did you learn all the stuff I taught you about the solar system?

(a) Yes (b) No

If your answer is yes, I will take your word for it.

There is no reason for anyone's head to blow up.

Thank you.

From your teacher friend,

Junie B. Jones

REPORT CARDS (GULP!)

REPORT CARDS are the worriest cards there ~~is.~~ are

Report cards are when teachers **ADD UP** the grades from **ALL** your homework and **ALL** your quizzes and **ALL** your tests.

Then they figure up a **GRADE** in **EVERY SINGLE SUBJECT.** And they put the **GRADES** on A REPORT CARD.

But **THAT** is not the worst part. 'Cause then they make you take the report card home to Mother and Daddy!

Is that **REALLY NECESSARY,** do you think?

If you're not doing good at school, can't they just say, PLEASE DO BETTER and let it go at that?

Also—to **prove** that Mother and Daddy saw it—you have to have them SIGN IT and bring it back! That is JUST PLAIN INSULTING, I tell you!

(Helpful hint: Do not try to hide your report card in your shirt. On account of a report card is very bulky, and Mother and Daddy can see the shape poking through.)

This is more information I learned the hard way.

ALSO . . .

Do **NOT** bury your report card in **GROUCHY MRS. MORTY'S** yard and then cover it up with dirt. On account of GROUCHY MRS. MORTY is ALWAYS, ALWAYS, ALWAYS snooping out of her window. And that BIG PEEKER will call your mother before you can even get home and explain yourself!

This is the real actual size of GROUCHY MRS. MORTY'S head.
REPORT CARD

OKAY . . .

So here is the **LAST WARNING** I want to give you about REPORT CARDS.

Teachers give you a GRADE IN ~~BEHAVYER~~ BEHAVIOR.

I am **NOT** kidding . . . BEHAVIOR!!!

(I do not actually want to discuss my grades in behavior at this time.)

BUT!

I **DO** want to discuss MY MOTHER'S GRADES IN BEHAVIOR!

'Cause **this** is a story I've been waiting for ALL MY LIFE!

A FUNNY STORY ABOUT MOTHER'S REPORT CARD!

by Junie B. Jones

One day Mother was cleaning out the closet. Then—all of a sudden—she did a loud squeal.

MY REPORT CARD! MY REPORT CARD! I FOUND MY OLD REPORT CARD! she hollered real loud.

Then she ran **SPEEDY QUICK** to the kitchen. And she took it out for Daddy to see!

He picked me up so I could see, too!

Then all of us looked at it together.

Pretty soon, Daddy's mouth came open.

WHOA! he said.

Mother's eyes got biggish and roundish.
Oh my, I didn't remember that, she said.

I did a **GASP!**

Then I shouted **REAL LOUD!**

HEY! WHAT DO YOU KNOW! MOTHER DID NOT BEHAVE HERSELF EITHER!!!

Daddy quick put me down.

I danced and danced.

And I laughed and laughed.

And I sang a happy song.

It was called **MOTHER WAS A BAD KID.**

After my song, I got marched to my room.

It was **A Delightful Day!**

The End

(I taped Mother's report card on the next two pages. That thing just makes me smile and smile.)

NAME Miller (Last) Susan (First) B. (Middle) H. R. 9

MARKING KEY: A—Excellent, Superior Work; B—Good; C—Fair or Average; D—Below Average, Warning Grade; E—Failing. In Grades 1 - 6, Special Subject Marks: S—Satisfactory; U—Unsatisfactory; I—Improving.

SUBJECTS	PHASES OF WORK EMPHASIZED	TRAITS	MARKS OCT.	DEC.	FEB.	APR.	JUNE
Reading	Comprehension, expression, interest, habits, use of reference books, and reading level.	ACHIEVEMENT	B	A	A	A	A
		EFFORT					
		CONDUCT					
English	Literature, grammar, oral and written expression, and speaking poise.	ACHIEVEMENT					
		EFFORT					
		CONDUCT					
Arithmetic	Computation, reasoning, care, accuracy, checking, retention, and written work.	ACHIEVEMENT	A	A	A	A	A
		EFFORT	B	B	B	B	B
		CONDUCT	C	C	C	C	C
Soc. Stu.	Use of facts, contribution to recitation, use of reference material, and written work.	ACHIEVEMENT	B	B	B	B	B
		EFFORT					
		CONDUCT					
Geography	Use of facts, contribution to recitation, use of reference material, and written work.	ACHIEVEMENT					
		EFFORT					
		CONDUCT					
Spelling	Accuracy, habits, recognition of difficulties, meaning of words, and dictionary use.	ACHIEVEMENT					
		EFFORT					
		CONDUCT					
Writing	Legibility, neatness, and application to other work.	ACHIEVEMENT	B	B	B	B	B
		EFFORT					
		CONDUCT					
Music	Participation, growth, enjoyment, and appreciation.	ACHIEVEMENT	S	S	S	S	S
		EFFORT					
		CONDUCT					
Fine Arts	Expression, handling of material, growth, enjoyment, and appreciation.	ACHIEVEMENT	S	S	S	S	S
		EFFORT					
		CONDUCT					
Manual Arts	Handling of tools and material, desire to design and make things, and value of products made.	ACHIEVEMENT					
		EFFORT					
		CONDUCT					
Physical Education	Interest in health and physical development, and ability to participate with others.	ACHIEVEMENT	S	S	S	S	S
		EFFORT					
		CONDUCT					
Science	Application of facts, class participation, and project work.	ACHIEVEMENT					
		EFFORT					
		CONDUCT					

C is average

SCHOOL Brainerd Elem. GRADE 1 19 83 19 84

COMMENTS OF THE HOME ROOM TEACHER

FIRST MARKING PERIOD

Susan is alert and attentive. She follows directions well. She expresses ideas well and takes an active part in our group discussions. At times she talks too much to her neighbors.

Signature Jeanette A. Martin

SECOND MARKING PERIOD

Susan is doing satisfactory work but at times she becomes careless.

Signature Jeanette A. Martin

THIRD MARKING PERIOD

Satisfactory work. We are trying to help Susan remember not to talk when someone else is talking.

Signature Jeanette A. Martin

FOURTH MARKING PERIOD

Satisfactory.

Signature Jeanette A. Martin

FIFTH MARKING PERIOD

Susan has done some satisfactory work this year. She gets along well with others. Susan has the ability to express her ideas clearly and always takes an active part in group discussions.

Signature Jeanette A. Martin

Susan should continue to practice her letters. Capital A-Z
small a-z

HOMEWORK THAT YOU MIGHT LOVE, LOVE, LOVE

It was fun thinking of FUNWORK I would love. I can think of lots more, I bet.

Like . . . hmm . . . I would like to WATCH CARTOONS ALL NIGHT! AND BUY A NEW PUPPY! AND TICKLE MY GRAMPA SILLY!

I bet you would like drawing your own FUNWORK, too! And so here are 2 spaces for you!

FUNWORK #1!

FUNWORK #2!

Plus HERE is a page for you to make up your very own EASY TEST!

(I already gave you an A+ of course!)

EASY TEST

A+

SECTION 6

GETTING SMILEY

(New friends and other happy stuff!)

FRIENDS YOU WILL LIKE . . . PROBABLY
(Plus Some You Won't Actually Care For)

At school, you will make a LOT of new friends.

New friends are the **HAPPIEST** part of school . . . usually.

Only here is a little bit of a problem.

On the first day of school, new friends are **NOT** actually friends yet.

They are still **strangers**.

And **strangers** are **STRANGE.**

I get nervous on the first day of school.

This year—while I was eating my breakfast—my stomach got flutterflies in it.

Also, it got buzzy bees.

After I finished breakfast, I jumped down from my chair and I ran around the kitchen.

STRANGERS! STRANGERS! I'VE GOT TO MEET STRANGERS! I shouted real loud.

That's how come Daddy quick picked me up.

And he took me to a quiet place.

And he told me some words of ~~wisedom~~ wisdom.

There is no reason to be nervous about strangers in your class, Junie B. Strangers are just new friends who you haven't met yet, he said.

After that, he put me back down.

And he smiled very nice.

I stared at him a real long time.

Who do you think you're kidding, Bob? I said.

Daddy stopped smiling.

I went to my room for a time out.

I am not allowed to call him Bob.

AND SO HERE IS WHAT HAPPENED AFTER MY TIME OUT . . .

Mother got me dressed.
And Daddy took me to my new first grade class.

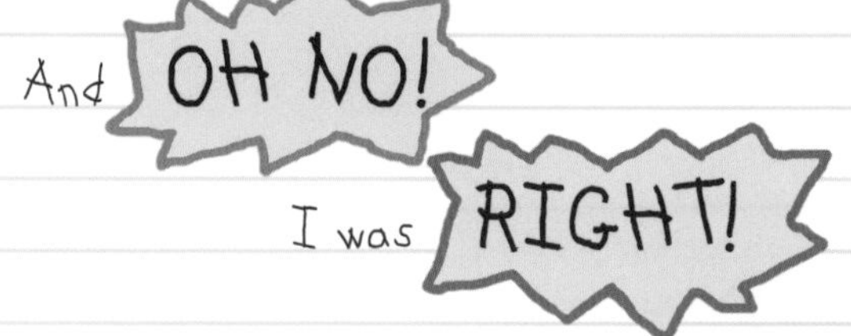

The room was FULL of **STRANGERS!**

But **GOOD NEWS!**
'Cause Daddy turned out to be even MORE RIGHT than me!
On account of ALL of those STRANGERS turned into FRIENDS before I even knew it!

I cannot even explain it!
That is just what happens at school!

I met FIVE brand new friends
in ONE single day!

(Also, I met Tattletale May. But I will ~~disgust~~ discuss that later.)

A boy named Herb turned out to be my bestest friend.
He sits at the desk in front of me.
Herb understands me **no matter what.**
That is just PLAIN NICE.

Here is Herbert's hair and ears. I traced it off his school picture.

(I am not actually good at tracing faces. I am only good at hair and ears.)

All of my friends have different hair and ears. I never actually noticed that situation before.

Here are other friends who sit near me, too.

Their names are 

hair and ears

and 

hair and ears

and Sheldon's hair and ears.

Plus here is just Shirley's hair. (On account of Shirley's ears don't actually appear that much.)

But . . . AHA!

Now **here is MAY'S** hair and ears!
Just **look** at that, would you?
That hair does not even
LOOK friendly.

May's hair looks like SNOOPYHEAD HAIR!
And that SNOOP sits right directly next to me!

Sitting next to May was the **worstest luck** I ever heard of.
Only I am not allowed to keep complaining about it.
On account of Grampa Miller says that **life does not always have good seating ~~arangments~~ arrangements**.

Grampa also says that sometimes—if you smile at people who aren't nice—it will make them smile back.

That is how come I went to school.
And I started grinning at May
VERY, VERY BIG.

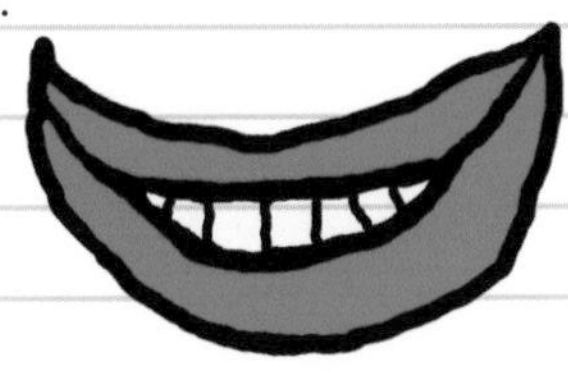

It did not work out that well.
May said if I didn't stop grinning she was going to call the police.

That is all I want to say about May.

But YAY! Here is something GOOD you should know about FRIENDS.

And it is called, sometimes you will start out NOT liking someone at school.

But then something happens.

And you end up liking them VERY, VERY MUCH!

That happened to me in kindergarten last year.

I did not like a boy named MEANIE JIM.

And he did not like me right back!

Only here is some SHOCKING news I found out!

All the time Meanie Jim was pretending not to like me . . .

he really, really LOVED me!

I am NOT kidding!

Jim gave me the most beautiful valentime I ever even saw!

It looked kind of like this.

Only it came from a real actual heart store!

And so after that,

me and Jim lived HAPPILY EVER AFTER!

OKAY. So here ~~is~~ are 3 THINGS I have learned about people at school . . .

1. There are people who I will like.
2. There are other people who I won't actually care for.
3. Plus there are other people who won't care for me. (That one is hard to believe.)

BUT . . .

OOPS!

WAIT!

I ALMOST FORGOT!

There is a **THING NUMBER FOUR!**

4. 'Cause sometimes you will have a bestest good friend **ONE** year. But the **NEXT** year, the school will put you in 2 DIFFERENT classrooms.

I am **NOT** kidding!

That is exactly what happened with my **bestest friend from kindergarten.**

Her name was That Grace.

That Grace had the CUTEST HAIR I ever saw. It was called automatically curly.

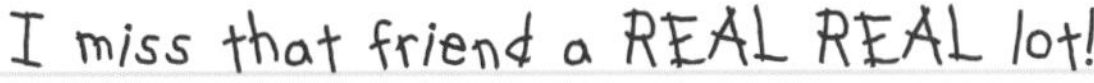
I miss that friend a REAL REAL lot!

BUT that is not **ALL** the news about my old friends in kindergarten . . .

On account of my other bestest friend was named Richie Lucille.

And this year me and Richie Lucille got put in the **SAME EXACT CLASS** again!

Only what do you know?

Lucille said she did not actually **want** to be friends with me again.

She said I already got my chance with her **last year.** And **this year** she had to give someone **else** a turn.

That is how come I ended up finding my **NEW FRIENDS** named HERBERT and LENNIE and JOSÉ and SHELDON and SHIRLEY.

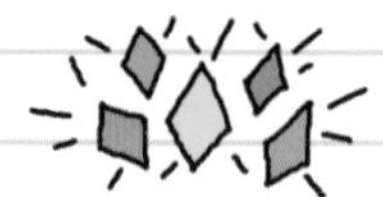

And those friends are **GEMS** I tell you!

So here is what I learned . . .

Sometimes NEW FRIENDS work out **EVEN BETTER** than OLD FRIENDS!

HA!

THAT IS JUST DELIGHTFUL!

THREE OTHER THINGS THAT MAKE ME SMILEY

1. THE PENCIL SHARPENER

The pencil sharpener is an interesting classroom item.

A pencil sharpener can take a roundy little pencil nub and make it as sharpy as it can be.

But THAT is NOT why it makes me SMILEY!

The REASON the pencil sharpener makes me smiley is because it gives me a way to get **out of my seat!**

Here is how the operation works . . .

Step 1. First I am working and working on my work.

Step 2. Then I start getting squirmy with ants in my pants.

I stop to take a breather.

Then I look down at my pencil.

And BINGO!

If I am LUCKY . . .

That thing is a ROUNDY NUB!

Step 3. I raise my hand very polite. Then I holler

MY PENCIL IS A ROUNDY NUB!

Step 4. Mr. Scary frowns his eyebrows at me.

I keep on waving my pencil.

Then YAY!

He FINALLY lets me go to **the pencil sharpener!**

And THAT gets the **ants** right out of my pants!

2. THE LAVATORY

The lavatory is the second thing that makes me smiley.

Lavatory is the school word for bathroom.

Don't ask me why.

It is another mystery about school words.

The lavatory has mirrors and sinks.

Also it has a nice assortment of toilets.

But that is no big whoop.

And so **HERE** is the **REASON** it makes me **SMILEY!**

THE LAVATORY gives me ANOTHER reason to get **out of my seat!**

Here is how it works . . .

Step 1. First I am working and working on my work.

Step 2. Then I start getting squirmy with ants in my pants.

I stop to take a breather.

Then I look down at my pencil.

And **BAD NEWS!**

It is **NOT a ROUNDY NUB!**

Step 3. I raise my hand very polite. Then I holler,

I NEED TO GO TO THE LAVATORY!

AND I AM **SERIOUSLY NOT KIDDING THIS TIME!**

Step 4. Usually I get frowned at again.

But I **almost always** get a lavatory pass.

And sometimes a lavatory pass is just the **break from work** that a little child needs.

A FUN LAVATORY STORY

One time, me and my friend Shirley got a Bathroom Buddy Pass to go to THE LAVATORY.
That means we can go together.
We had a very fun adventure. On account of me and her had a CONTEST to see who could wash our hands the longest.

We washed and washed and washed!

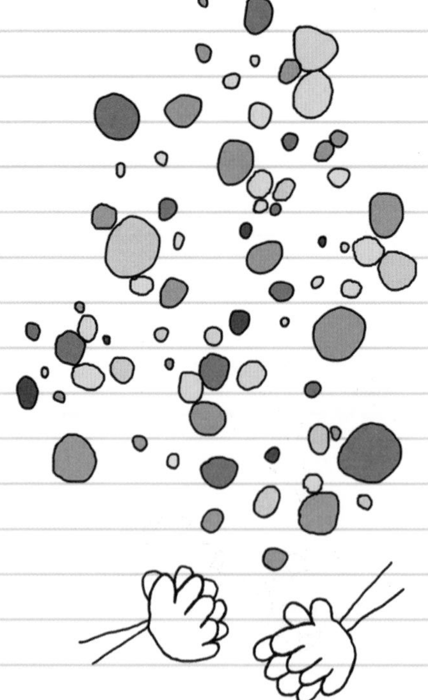

Then finally Mr. Scary sent May to get us.
Now Shirley and I cannot be BATHROOM BUDDIES anymore.
That is unfortunate.

3. THE WATER FOUNTAIN

HURRAY!

THE WATER FOUNTAIN is the third thing that makes me SMILEY!

The story starts the same old way . . .

Step 1. First I am working and working on my work.

Step 2. Then I get the same exact ants in my pants.

So I stop to take a breather.

And then I look over at May.

And—just as a funny joke—I give her a teensy poke with my pencil nub eraser.

Only BIG SURPRISE.

May does not think that is amusing.

And she tattletales to the teacher.

And **he** sends me to **The Office.**

And I have to have a **discussion** with **Principal.**

(**Discussion** is the school word for why did you poke May with your pencil nub?)

Step 3. After it is over, I walk back to class very glum.

I am feeling saddish and slumpish.

Also my mouth is dryish from all that discussion.

Step 4. And then—all of a sudden—

I look down the hall . . . and

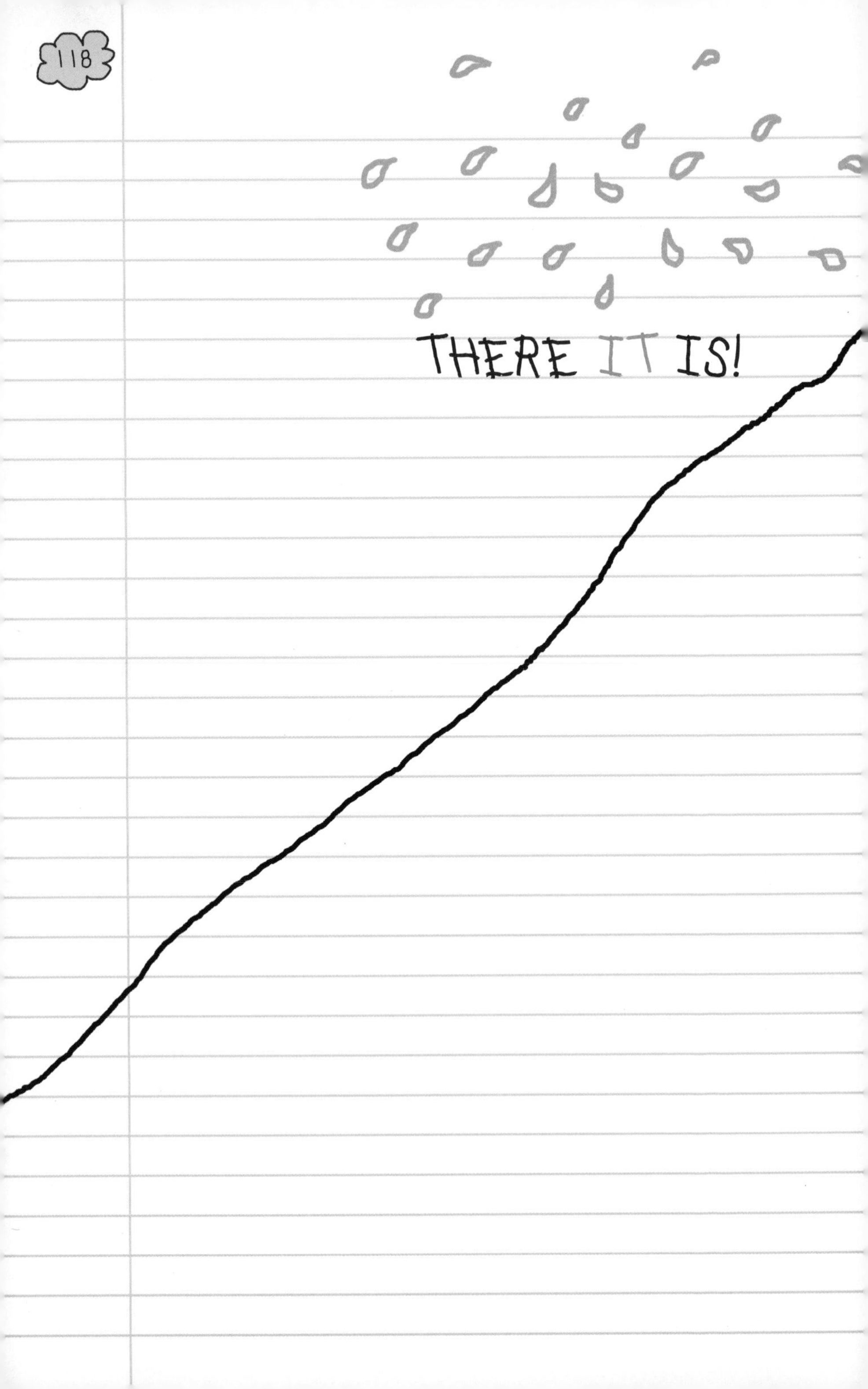
THERE IT IS!

THE WATER FOUNTAIN

And that thing feels like A FRIEND, I tell you!

Step 5. I run to the fountain speedy fast. Then I turn on its little bubble spout. And I drink cold water until my lips get chilly!

Step 6. After that, I go back to my room with chilly dribble drops on my chin. And I feel ready to start being good all over again . . . possibly. (Or maybe not.)

But whoever invented THE WATER FOUNTAIN is MY HERO!

And that is the truth!

THE HAPPIEST LAST THINGS IN MY GUIDE TO SCHOOL!

All rightie . . . this is IT!

This is the VERY LAST STUFF I wanted to tell you about.

But it is the HAPPIEST stuff of all, I think.

'Cause it is all about my FAVORITE SMELLS at school.

Grampa Miller says that **good smells** can make you like ANY PLACE. (almost)

And so sometimes—when I really REALLY do NOT WANT TO GO TO SCHOOL—I think of my 3 FAVORITE SMELLS at that place.

And then BOOM!

I can't wait to get on the

And so HERE THEY ARE . . .

MY 3 FAVORITE SMELLS AT SCHOOL!

(1) FIRST, I like the smell of GRASS on the playground right after Gus Vallony gets finished mowing it.

That smell makes me want to breathe and breathe.

(2) NEXT, I like the SMELL OF BRAND NEW CRAYONS when I come to school after summer vacation. New crayons smell all fresh and pointy.

(3) BUT MOSTLY I LOVE the smell of the WHOLE ENTIRE BUILDING when the cafeteria is baking

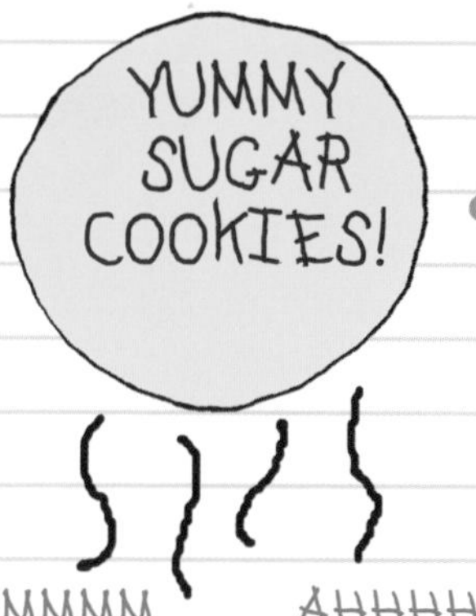

MMMMM . . . AHHHHH!
That smell makes me wish I was at school
RIGHT EXACTLY NOW!
Yum . . . I am going to keep on smelling them in my head until school starts tomorrow, I think!

Hey! Maybe I will see you there!
We could have the TIME OF OUR LIFE, I bet!

But even if I don't see you . . . I hope you have FUN there, okay? (And I hope my SCHOOL GUIDE helped!)

GOOD LUCK and HAPPY SCHOOL!
The End

Junie B., First Grader

THE LAST SPACE IN MY BOOK!

Look! I saved the LAST PAGES of my book for Y-O-U!

Here are some little frames where you can draw your own friends' hair and ears!

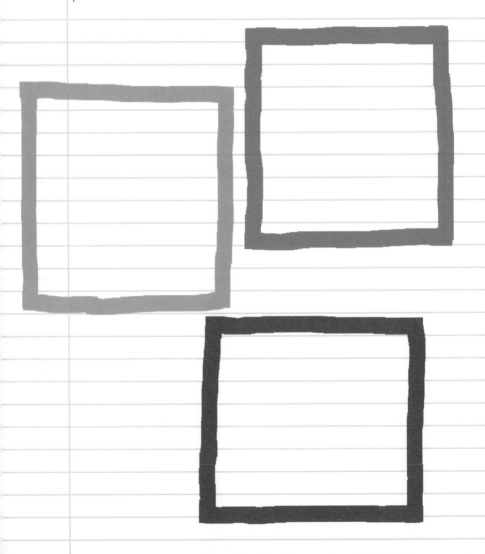

And now . . . TA DAA!!!
Here it REALLY is!
THE VERY LAST SPACE YOU GET TO DRAW IN!
And guess what?
You can draw ANY HAPPY THING about school you want!

THE END

JUNIE B. JONES is a first grader at Clarence somebody or other Elementary School. Her birthday is Junie the first. She lives with Mother, Daddy, her dog named Tickle, and her little brother named Ollie. She enjoys plumbing supplies, cheese sandwiches, and lemon pie. Her best friend is Herb. And her favorite color is she is not actually sure.

GRAMPA FRANK MILLER lives with his lovely wife, Helen, and Helen's pet bird, Twitter. He enjoys fishing, fixing the toilet, and spending time with his favorite grandgirl, Junie B. Jones.

BARBARA PARK is beloved by millions as the author of the wildly popular, *New York Times* bestselling Junie B. Jones series. She has won over forty children's book awards and has been featured in the *New York Times*, *USA Today*, and *Time* magazine. With fifty million copies in print in more than a dozen languages, the Junie B. Jones books are a staple in classrooms everywhere and have kept kids laughing—and reading—for over twenty years. Barbara says, "I've never been sure whether Junie B.'s fans love her in spite of her imperfections . . . or because of them. But either way, she's gone out into the world and made more friends than I ever dreamed possible."

Barbara Park is also the author of award-winning middle-grade novels and bestselling picture books, including *The Kid in the Red Jacket*, *Mick Harte Was Here*, and *MA! There's Nothing to Do Here!* She and her husband, Richard, live in Arizona. Her family—which now includes two of the handsomest little grandboys on the planet—lives nearby.

Laugh yourself silly with Junie B.!

BARBARA PARK
Junie B. Jones
Is a
Graduation Girl

BARBARA PARK
Junie B., First Grader
(at last!)

BARBARA PARK
Junie B., First Grader
Boss of Lunch

BARBARA PARK
Junie B., First Grader
Toothless Wonder

BARBARA PARK
Junie B., First Grader
Cheater Pants

BARBARA PARK
Junie B., First Grader
One-Man Band

BARBARA PARK
TOP-SECRET
Personal Beeswax
A Journal by Junie B.
(and me!)

BARBARA PARK
Junie B., First Grader
Shipwrecked

BARBARA PARK
Junie B., First Grader
BOO...and I MEAN It!

BARBARA PARK
Junie B., First Grader
Jingle Bells, Batman Smells!
(P.S. So Does May.)

BARBARA PARK
Junie B., First Grader
Aloha-ha-ha!

BARBARA PARK
Junie B., First Grader
Dumb Bunny

BARBARA PARK
Junie B.'s Essential
Survival Guide to School

BARBARA PARK
Junie B.'s
These Puzzles Hurt My Brain!
BOOK

BARBARA PARK
Junie B., First Grader
Turkeys We Have Loved
and Eaten
(and Other Thankful Stuff)

This is a work of fiction. Names, characters, places, and incidents either are the product of the author's imagination or are used fictitiously. Any resemblance to actual persons, living or dead, events, or locales is entirely coincidental.

Published in the United States by Random House Children's Books, a division of Random House, Inc., New York. Originally published in a spiral-bound edition by Random House Children's Books, New York, in 2009.

Random House and the colophon are registered trademarks and A Stepping Stone Book and the colophon are trademarks of Random House, Inc. Junie B., First Grader® stylized design is a registered trademark of Barbara Park, used under license.

Visit us on the Web! randomhouse.com/kids/junieb

Educators and librarians, for a variety of teaching tools, visit us at RHTeachersLibrarians.com

The Library of Congress has cataloged an earlier edition of this work with the Library of Congress Control Number 2008925171

ISBN 978-0-449-81783-4 (hardcover) — ISBN 978-0-375-83811-8 (spiral-bound)

MANUFACTURED IN CHINA 10 9 8 7 6 5 4 3 2 1
First Hardcover Edition 2013

Random House Children's Books supports the First Amendment and celebrates the right to read.

NOTEBOOK
purple
blue
green